HOTEL FANTASTIC

THOMAS GIBAULT

KIDS CAN PRESS

To Sanam-joon. And to the Tluabig, Ailgarrom, Éttoc, Nohguop and Sdohg,
I will always have a room ready for you at Hotel Fantastic

Text and illustrations © 2018 Thomas Gibault

Kids Can Press gratefully acknowledges the financial support of the Government of Ontario, through the Ontario Media Development Corporation; the Ontario Arts Council; the Canada Council for the Arts; and the Government of Canada, through the CBF, for our publishing activity.

Published in Canada and the U.S. by Kids Can Press Ltd.
25 Dockside Drive, Toronto, ON M5A 0B5

Kids Can Press is a Corus Entertainment Inc. company

www.kidscanpress.com

The artwork in this book was rendered digitally in Photoshop.
The text is set in Caslon.

Edited by Jennifer Stokes
Designed by Marie Bartholomew

Printed and bound in Malaysia, in 3/2018 by Tien Wah Press (Pte.) Ltd.

CM 18 0 9 8 7 6 5 4 3 2 1

Library and Archives Canada Cataloguing in Publication

Gibault, Thomas, 1982–, author, illustrator
Hotel Fantastic / Thomas Gibault.

ISBN 978-1-77138-992-1 (hardcover)

I. Title.

PS8613.I278H68 2018   jC813'.6   C2017-908034-2

You're guaranteed to enjoy your stay at Hotel Fantastic. It's a place like no other.

No matter who you are or where you're from, you'll find a room perfectly suited to a good night's sleep.

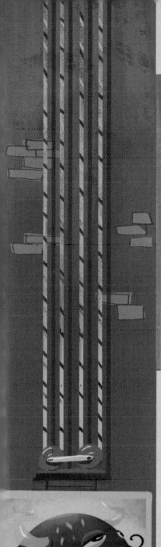

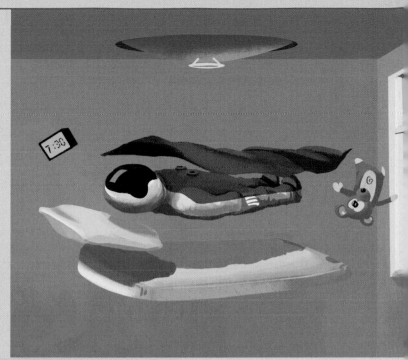

Those who fly will have access to the Sky Rooms.

Are you interested in bringing home a souvenir?
The hotel gift shop is just the place.

Our restaurant is world-famous. Come to the second floor to taste the delicious cuisine of Raymundo and Georgio!

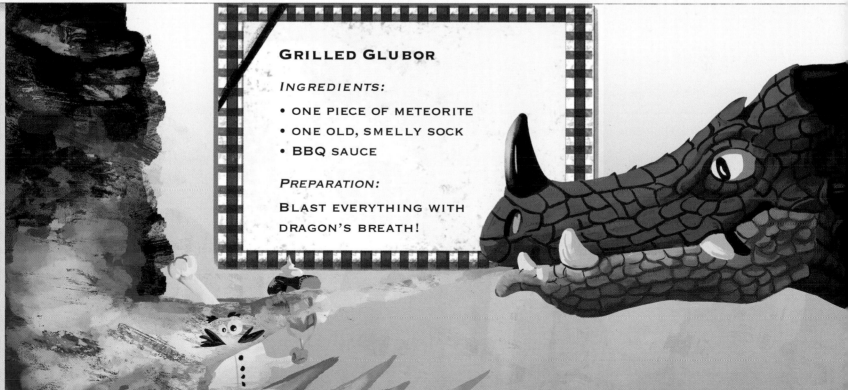

GRILLED GLUBOR

INGREDIENTS:

- ONE PIECE OF METEORITE
- ONE OLD, SMELLY SOCK
- BBQ SAUCE

PREPARATION:

BLAST EVERYTHING WITH
DRAGON'S BREATH!

For your convenience, we have a fully equipped gym!

Don't be afraid to work up a sweat.

Powerful vacuums whisk away unwanted smells.

Our rooftop swimming
pool is available to all.

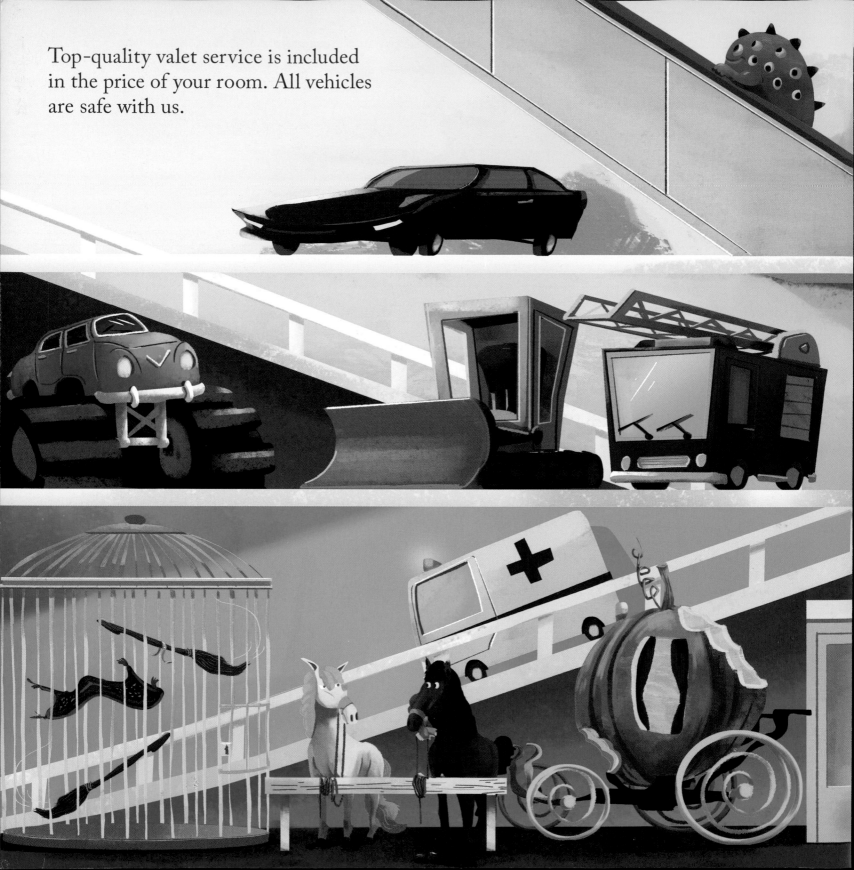

Top-quality valet service is included in the price of your room. All vehicles are safe with us.

GALACTIC PORTAL

LOBBY

1

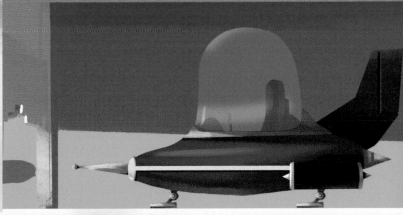

2

WANTED!

3

If you feel like dancing, the basement ballroom is open all hours of the day and night.

Do you have aches and pains? One stop at our infirmary, and you'll be back on your feet in no time.

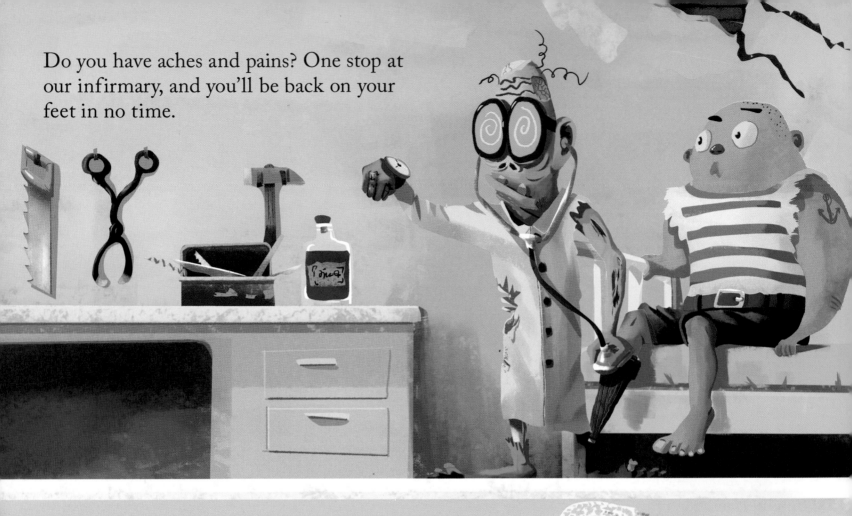

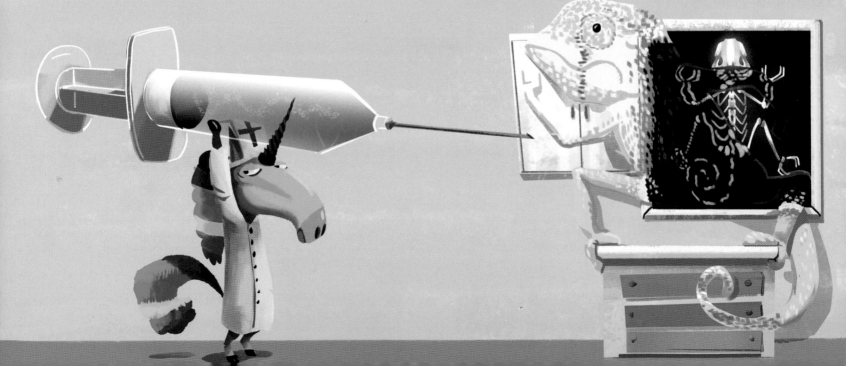

You may even be given some upgrades!

Cyborg eye

Octopus arm

Flippered foot

Supersonic rocket-feet

Multifunction hand

Hotel security is our top priority. Our elite strike team is always ready for action.

But even these security
specialists are no match for
SOROR-HORRIBILIS!